long night moon

long night moon

by cynthia rylant
illustrated by mark siegel

SIMON & SCHUSTER BOOKS FOR YOUNG READERS
New York   London   Toronto   Sydney

Long ago Native Americans
gave names to the full moons
they watched throughout the year.
Each month had a moon.
And each moon had its name. . . .

In January
the Stormy Moon shines
in mist,
in ice,
on a wild wolf's back.

Find it
and find your way home.

In February
a Snow Moon glows

white,

sharp,

in a cool,
crackling
breath.

It will miss
its sister, the Sun.

In March
a Sap Moon rises
over
melting ponds,
sleepy bears,
small green trees.

It tells a promise
and a hope.

In April
the Sprouting Grass Moon brings
all wanderers back home.

Baby birds love this moon.
It lights their tiny heads.

In May
a Flower Moon blooms
wide open,
bright.

Happy to be here.

It is a smiling moon.
It is a song.

In June
the Strawberry Moon shimmers
on succulent buds,
on crisp new shoots,
on quiet, grateful rabbits.

There is
in the dark
a moonlight meal.

In July
the Thunder Moon trembles,
shudders,
and disappears
in a thick   black   sky.

It listens to the
clouds
beat their drums.

In August
a Harvest Moon grows

round

and

full

like a big ripe melon,
blessing the calm fields of hay.

In September
a Coon Moon watches
for shining eyes and busy feet,
little brown noses in the air.

It loves the small
night creatures.

It shows them
a better

path.

In October
the Acorn Moon comes
strong,
yellow.
The biggest moon of the year.
Leaves are falling and birds are flying.

This moon says good-bye.

In November a Frosty Moon holds

a hard ground,

empty trees,

the wind in lonely places.

It shivers with the shining stars.

It thinks it might

just

sleep.

And in December
the Long Night Moon waits

and waits

and waits

for morning.

This
is the faithful moon.

This one is your friend.

The Adventure of Illustrating *Long Night Moon*

The beauty and simple grace of Cynthia Rylant's *Long Night Moon* captivated me immediately. In her lyrical tribute to the Native American tradition of naming the full moons, I felt the author captured not just one, but many moods of night. To me these distinct atmospheres seemed best explored in one continuous 360-degree panorama over the course of a year.

But finding the right medium proved to be a challenge. I tried acrylics and then oils, but nothing came close to rendering the magic of Cynthia's words. Then I went outside. Over several months I took many long walks by moonlight in the beautiful Rockefeller Farms, near Sleepy Hollow, New York. In my busy, crowded life, I'd never given so much attention to moonlight: What is it like? How does it feel? What makes it so special? Eventually — and almost accidentally — charcoal revealed itself as the medium of choice. It returned me to that velvety mysterious light that softens everything, bathing nature in a dreamy luminosity.

I realize now how tempting it is to think that nature closes up shop after sunset, but this isn't so. When the sun goes down, nature doesn't disappear. She shows us another face, one that is just as complex and astonishing as the face she wears during the day. When we are young children, night sometimes has a forbidding, or even forbidden quality — it is, after all, time for bed. But its attraction is no less powerful. May the words and images of *Long Night Moon* offer a safe invitation to savor the night and celebrate its otherwise hidden wonders.—M. S.

SIMON & SCHUSTER BOOKS FOR YOUNG READERS

An imprint of Simon & Schuster Children's Publishing Division

1230 Avenue of the Americas, New York, New York 10020

Text copyright © 2004 by Cynthia Rylant

Illustrations copyright © 2004 by Mark Siegel

SIMON & SCHUSTER BOOKS FOR YOUNG READERS is a trademark of Simon & Schuster, Inc.

Book design by Mark Siegel

The text for this book is set in Wendy.

The illustrations are rendered in charcoal, pencil, and pastel on Arches paper and digital color.

Manufactured in China

10 9 8 7 6 5 4 3 2 1

Library of Congress Cataloging-in-Publication Data

Rylant, Cynthia.

Long night moon / Cynthia Rylant ; illustrated by Mark Siegel.

p. cm.

Summary: Text and illustrations depict the varied seasonal full moons that change and assume personalities of their own throughout the year.

ISBN 0-689-85426-9

[1. Moon—Phases—Fiction. 2. Seasons—Fiction. 3. Months—Fiction.

4. Indians of North America—Fiction.] I. Siegel, Mark, 1967– ill. II. Title.

PZ7.R982 Lo 2004   [E]—dc21   2002036492

For Aidan — C. R.

For Alexis — M. S.